j CHAPTER BK Mews M.
Mews, Melody,
The un-fairy /
9781534466449

12/2020

Itty ♥ Bitty
PRINCESS
⤜ Kitty ⤝

The Un-Fairy

by Melody Mews   illustrated by Ellen Stubbings

LITTLE SIMON

New York London Toronto Sydney New Delhi

LITTLE SIMON

An imprint of Simon & Schuster Children's Publishing Division
1230 Avenue of the Americas, New York, New York 10020
First Little Simon hardcover edition December 2020. Copyright © 2020 by Simon & Schuster, Inc. All rights reserved, including the right of reproduction in whole or in part in any form. LITTLE SIMON is a registered trademark of Simon & Schuster, Inc., and associated colophon is a trademark of Simon & Schuster, Inc. For information about special discounts for bulk purchases, please contact Simon & Schuster Special Sales at 1-866-506-1949 or business@simonandschuster.com.
The Simon & Schuster Speakers Bureau can bring authors to your live event.
For more information or to book an event contact the Simon & Schuster Speakers Bureau at 1-866-248-3049 or visit our website at www.simonspeakers.com.
Designed by Laura Roode. The text of this book was set in Banda.
Manufactured in the United States of America 1020 FFG 10 9 8 7 6 5 4 3 2 1
Library of Congress Cataloging-in-Publication Data
Names: Mews, Melody, author. | Stubbings, Ellen, illustrator. Title: The un-fairy / by Melody Mews ; illustrated by Ellen Stubbings. Description: First Little Simon paperback edition. | New York : Little Simon, 2020. | Series: Itty Bitty Princess Kitty ; 6 | Audience: Ages 5 - 9. | Audience: Grades K-1. | Summary: Itty Bitty Princess Kitty helps her new friend, Bree, to find her true fairy calling. Identifiers: LCCN 2019055175 | ISBN 9781534466432 (paperback) | ISBN 9781534466449 (hardcover) | ISBN 9781534466456 (eBook) Subjects: CYAC: Cats—Fiction. | Animals—Infancy—Fiction. | Princesses—Fiction. | Fairies—Fiction. | Fantasy. Classification: LCC PZ7.1.M4976 Un 2020 | DDC [E]—dc23
LC record available at https://lccn.loc.gov/2019055175

Contents

The
Food Fairies

It was dinnertime in Lollyland, and Itty Bitty Princess Kitty was hiding in one of her favorite places in the palace—the royal kitchen!

"Peaches, are you adding *marshmallows*?" Itty whispered.

Itty wasn't supposed to be there, but Peaches was a very

friendly fairy. The other fairies weren't *mean* . . . they just didn't like to be bothered, especially Garbanzo, the head food fairy.

Peaches looked over at Garbanzo, who was making a

soufflé. There were tiny spice bottles all over the counter.

"Yes, it's a *fairy* secret," Peaches squeaked. She flew over and gave Itty a fairy-size cup. "Here, have a taste!"

Itty sipped the soup. "It's so tasty!" she exclaimed.

"Does it need more sugar or salt?" Peaches asked.

"Nope!" Itty assured her. "It's perfect."

Peaches happily flew back to the pot. Then as she struggled to pick up a giant spoon, another fairy rushed over.

"Thanks, Bree!" Peaches cried.

"Of course!" the fairy squeaked before flying away.

Just moments later, a loud crash shook the kitchen. A bowl of pudding fell over, and Bree was now covered in brown goo. Itty quickly grabbed some towels, but Peaches stopped her.

"You should leave now, Prin—"

But it was too late! Garbanzo noticed Itty right away.

"Uh-oh," Itty mumbled.

"Princess Itty, you shouldn't be in here!" cried Garbanzo. "Please leave while we clean up. And, Bree, we need to talk."

Itty didn't care about the mess. She was happy to help clean up. But as she watched the fairies, Itty decided it would be best to stay out of the way.

Dessert Disaster

"Dinner was extra tasty tonight," King Kitty boomed as he wiped his whiskers.

"Yes, I wonder what the food fairies put in the soup to make it so delicious!" the Queen, Itty's mom, agreed.

"The secret is *marshmallows!*"
Itty cried. "I watched Peaches
make the soup."

"Itty, you know the food fairies
don't like to be bothered," her
mom said gently.

"I know," Itty said, looking down
at her feet. "But it smells so good
in there."

"Oh, I know," the King chuckled.
"Garbanzo chased me out with a
rolling pin last week!"

The Queen shook her head as
Itty giggled.

"I wonder why the dessert is taking so long," Itty said. "Can I go check?"

"Itty," her mom began, "what did we just talk about?"

"I won't bother them!" Itty promised.

"Okay, but don't upset Garbanzo," her dad said with a wink.

Itty nodded and jumped down from her seat.

When she entered the kitchen, she saw that something was wrong. The room was filled with stinky smoke! Some fairies were busy waving towels near the smoke detector while others were spraying tiny cans of air freshener around the room.

"What's going on?" Itty asked
as soon as she found Peaches.

"Our newest food fairy burned
the dessert," Peaches replied.
"And Garbanzo is *fairy* upset!"

"Hmm, let me try talking to her," Itty said.

"No, I don't think that's a very good idea," Peaches warned.

But Itty had made up her mind. She was going to help fix this dessert disaster!

It's Just Dessert

Itty could hear Garbanzo shouting orders from across the room.

"Jellybean, cut up the strawberries! The royal family is waiting!" she yelled in a panic.

"No, don't worry about us!" Itty cried as she hurried over.

"Princess Itty, please wait in the dining room," Garbanzo squeaked. "We'll make a new dessert, and—"

"But we don't need one," Itty said. "Dinner was *so* yummy, and we're way too full."

"But, Princess Itty, dessert is *always* a part of your family dinner," Garbanzo insisted.

"Not today!" Itty cried while patting her tummy. Itty loved

dessert, but she didn't want the food fairies to worry.

"Well, if you're absolutely sure . . . ," Garbanzo said slowly.

"Oh, I'm positive!" Itty nodded.

"Okay, thank you, Princess Itty,"
Garbanzo replied with a sigh. But
then she turned to Bree. "Make
sure to clean up this mess!"

The little fairy nodded as her
cheeks turned red.

When Garbanzo left, Itty walked up to the fairy named Bree. She was the fairy who had helped Peaches lift the giant spoon.

"I'm so sorry, Princess Itty," Bree said shyly.

"It's okay!" Itty said as she waved her paw. "And don't worry. Garbanzo is always grumpy."

Bree giggled. But her smile quickly turned into a frown.

"What's wrong?" Itty asked.

"I *wanted* to work in the royal kitchen," Bree said. "But I'm not very good at this."

Itty considered this. All the fairies in Lollyland had different jobs. But she'd never thought about how they got those jobs in the first place! "Well, what kind of fairy do you think you're meant to be?" Itty asked.

"I have no idea," Bree replied with a shrug.

"Maybe I can help!" Itty exclaimed. "Together, we can find the *fairy* best job for you!"

"Oh, thank you, Princess Itty!" Bree cried. And just like that, her frown had turned into the brightest smile.

The Buzz in
Goodie Grove

The next morning Itty met her friends Luna Unicorn, Esme Butterfly, and Chipper Bunny at Goodie Grove. She had told them she had a special treat to share.

"Hi, Itty! What's the surprise?" Chipper asked.

"Yes, tell us, please!" Luna squealed as a bit of glitter puffed from her horn. Luna's horn blew glitter whenever she was excited.

That's when Bree fluttered up from behind a bush next to Chipper.

"I didn't take any syrup, I promise!" he exclaimed.

"Don't worry. She's not a syrup fairy." Itty laughed. "This is my new friend, Bree. She's the surprise!"

Itty then explained that she was helping Bree find her true fairy calling. Itty's friends were excited to meet a friendly new fairy, so they all decided to explore Goodie Grove together.

"Let's start with the syrup fairies!"
Chipper suggested. "If *I* was a fairy,
that would be my calling."

"Wow, that sounds like the
sweetest job ever," Bree said.

"Yes, all the fairies in Goodie Grove gather treats," Esme explained as they walked toward the syrup river. "This is the most delicious place ever!"

Just then, the head syrup fairy,
Nougat, darted over and held up
her hand.

"No swimming in the river!" she
yelled, looking right at Chipper.

Itty said hello and explained that they were helping Bree find her true fairy calling.

"Oh, I'd love to try my wing at being a syrup fairy!" Bree shouted happily.

"Fine, you're welcome to give it a try," Nougat said, after a long pause. "Waffles, can you and Lollipop bring us a bucket?"

A moment later, two fairies flew over with a bucket.

"It'll get *fairy* heavy, so it takes at least two fairies—" Nougat began.

But Bree easily grabbed the bucket with just one arm. So Nougat instructed her to take the bucket to the river, fill it, and bring it back to the pouring station.

Itty and her friends watched as Bree did as she was told. Everything was going great until she lost focus halfway to the pouring station.

Syrup splattered everywhere, covering them all in very thick, sticky goo.

"I'm so sorry!" Bree exclaimed.
But her apology was drowned
out by a loud squeak as all the
fairies scattered away.

What in the world is going on? Itty wondered.

And that's when she heard it. A buzzing sound was growing in the distance.

"Oh no!" Luna shrieked. "BEES! Run!"

BUZZ

chapter 5

A Fairy
Close Call

Itty's friends decided to go home after they got away from the bees, but Itty wasn't ready to give up. So they headed to their next stop, the Royal Museum.

When they got to the museum, a group of art fairies fluttered over.

"Princess Itty, it's wonderful to see you!" the head art fairy, Paisley, exclaimed.

Itty greeted them and introduced Bree to the other fairies. Then she told them why they were there.

"We'd love for you to see the newest treasure from the most brilliant sculptor of all time—Michelpigelo!" Paisley exclaimed.

Itty and Bree couldn't wait to see it, so they followed Paisley into the building. A large sculpture sat on a platform, covered by a tarp.

Paisley clapped his hands and six fairies instantly appeared. They lifted the tarp to reveal . . . a marble sculpture of a ballerina pig eating a candy apple!

"Isn't it *magnificent*?" Paisley asked.

Itty looked over at her friend. Bree suddenly had a little twinkle in her eye.

"May I get closer?" Bree asked excitedly.

"Yes, but please be *fairy* careful."

Bree nodded. But then she zoomed up so fast that she bumped her little nose right into it! The ballerina pig rocked back and forth on the platform . . . and then started to tip over!

Itty covered her eyes, afraid to
look. But there was no loud crash,
so she lifted her paws. Somehow,
Bree had flown underneath the
marble pig and was holding it up
with her back!

"Umm, a little help, please?"
Bree squeaked.

Itty and Paisley rushed up to help Bree. Together, they carefully rested the sculpture back on the ground.

"I'm sorry, but I don't think being an art fairy is your calling," Paisley said.

Bree nodded shyly in agreement.

Bree didn't look happy as they left the museum. "Princess Itty,

I don't think I *have* a true fairy calling," she said sadly.

Itty wasn't sure how to make her friend feel better. But she knew she couldn't give up.

A Special
Project

The next morning Itty settled in to her desk at school.

Their classroom was in the rainbow ring, so their desks changed colors every hour when the mermaids sang. It was the beginning of the day, so their desks were red.

"How was the Royal Museum?"
Luna asked Itty as she sat down.
Itty told Luna about the terrible
thing that *almost* happened.

"Oh, poor Bree," Luna said. "I hope she finds what she's meant to be."

"I know! There has to be a fairy job that's just right for her," Itty agreed as their teacher, Miss Sophia, walked in.

"Good morning, class," their teacher said with a smile. "Today we will be learning all about woodworking. And each of you will be creating your own wood sculpture."

A beaver in the back of the classroom raised his hand.

"Yes, Benjamin?" Miss Sophia asked.

"Um, I know how to build dams," Benjamin said. "Can that count as my project?"

"We can discuss that," Miss Sophia replied. "Everyone else, please begin drawing what you'd like to make."

Itty had a bunch of ideas—a rocking horse, a bookshelf, or maybe even a birdhouse. They all sounded cool, but none of them felt right.

I want to make a special present for someone, Itty thought. And that's when she thought of Garbanzo and all the spice bottles that were in the kitchen. A fairy-size spice rack would be *perfect*!

So Itty began to sketch it right
away. It needed to be big enough
to hold a lot, but small enough
for a fairy to carry.

Itty turned and whispered her idea to her best friend.

"Wow, I'm making a sign with my name on it for my room," Luna said. "Isn't a spice rack going to be really . . . complicated?"

Itty shrugged. Luna was probably right. But if she worked really hard, it would be the perfect gift for Garbanzo.

Fairy Forest

Itty spent the next few days working on her spice rack. But no matter how hard she tried, she couldn't figure out what size it needed to be. She tried sneaking into the kitchen to take a look at the spice drawer, but Garbanzo chased her out every time.

After several failed tries, Itty finally realized that she knew a fairy she could talk to.

And Itty knew exactly where to find her.

"Mom, Dad, I'm going to Fairy

Forest," Itty called as she ran down the royal stairs.

"Okay," her mom replied. "But remember not to bother the fairies!"

"I won't," Itty promised. Then she ran outside and hailed a cloud.

A few minutes later, Itty arrived at Fairy Forest. Right away she spotted a group of fairies under a bush.

Maybe they can help me find Bree, Itty thought. *I just hope they're not announcement fairies.* Announcement fairies were possibly the grumpiest fairies of all.

As Itty got closer, she saw they were typing on miniature typewriters. They were writer fairies.

"Excuse me," Itty said.

"Can't you see we're trying to write?" one of the fairies grumbled. But when she looked up, her face softened. "Oh, sorry, Princess Itty! Did you need something?"

Itty nodded and told them she was looking for Bree.

"I think she's in the garden," the fairy replied.

Itty said thank you and ran to the garden. Sure enough, Bree was sitting on a fairy bench by herself.

Bree's face lit up as soon as she saw Itty. "Princess Itty, what a nice surprise!"

"Hi, Bree! How come you're here all alone?" Itty asked.

"I haven't really made friends yet. I'm too worried about what I'm meant to be," Bree admitted.

"Don't worry. You'll figure it out soon," Itty replied. "And I'm your friend! From now on, just call me Itty."

Bree nodded, and then Itty told Bree about the gift for Garbanzo. Just as Luna had guessed, it was proving to be a pretty difficult project.

"Well, you're in luck!" Bree cried with excitement. "Because not only do I know exactly how many spice jars there are, I'm also *fairy* good at building things!"

A Fairy Helpful Friend

The next day after school Bree came to the palace to help Itty with her spice rack design. She knew exactly what changes it needed. Then she showed Itty how to measure, cut, and sand each piece of wood.

"I think I should start putting this

together," Itty said after cutting the last piece.

"Are you sure you don't want help?" Bree asked.

"Don't worry," Itty replied. "I know you have other fairy things to worry about."

"Oh, but this is fun," Bree said. "I'm happy to stay!"

So the two friends kept working, and in the end, Itty was glad that Bree was there. Because at one point, Itty glued one of the shelves

WHITE

RED

on backward. But Bree helped her fix it right away. And then, when Itty ran out of pink paint, Bree showed her how to mix more. Before they knew it, they had finished the project—and it wasn't even time for dinner!

"I couldn't have made this without you," Itty said when they were done. "How do you know how to do all this stuff?"

"I've always been good at building things," Bree replied. "I'm not clumsy when it comes to building . . . but I do seem to have trouble with *everything* else."

"Oh, don't be so hard on yourself," Itty said. "No one is good at *everything*! And you're not just *good* at building . . . you're GREAT!"

"Thanks, Itty." Bree smiled. "I guess it's too bad there aren't such things as *builder* fairies."

Itty gasped and jumped up. She finally knew *exactly* which fairies they needed to go see.

Builder
Fairies

"Builder fairies!" Itty cried as she danced around happily. "You *can* put your building skills to use! Mr. Bobtail, our royal architect, worked with a team of builder fairies to create my fancy bedroom when I became a princess."

"I can't believe I've never heard of them!" Bree exclaimed. "How do we meet these fairies?"

Itty knew that her dad would know, so they went to go see him in his royal office.

After knocking on the door, she told the King that Bree needed to see Mr. Bobtail to meet the builder fairies. Just as Itty expected, her dad knew exactly where to go: the new library in downtown Lollyland. With that, the two friends thanked the king and rushed out the door.

"Princess Itty, it is very nice to see you again," Mr. Bobtail said when Itty and Bree arrived.

"Yes, it sure is! And I brought my friend, Bree," Itty said. "She helped me build the most amazing spice rack made out of wood. I think she would be a great fit as a new builder fairy."

"Is that right?" the royal architect asked.

"Yes, sir," Bree replied. "I was *fairy* excited when Itty told me there were builder fairies in Lollyland. I never knew that was something I could do."

"That's because this is an *extremely* rare calling for a fairy. You have to be extra strong."

Bree threw her shoulders back and stood up to her full height of three inches. "Oh, I might be tiny, but I'm *fairy* strong!" she cried happily.

Itty knew Bree was right. From the first time the two friends met, Bree had shown her incredible strength. She had helped Peaches lift a giant spoon, she'd lifted the syrup bucket all by herself, and she had even caught that heavy marble sculpture at the Royal Museum.

All she needed to do was show Mr. Bobtail and the other fairies what she could do.

A Fairy Special Exception

Later that evening, Itty was having dinner with her parents when her dad had exciting news to share.

"I spoke to Mr. Bobtail," the King said as he brushed crumbs off his robe. "He said Bree is the best builder fairy he's ever seen!"

"Itty, it was very nice of you to help Bree find her true fairy calling," her mom purred. "I'm *fairy* proud of you."

Itty grinned. She had spoken to Bree, and it sounded like the other builder fairies had welcomed her with open wings. Itty was so happy for Bree. She not only found her true fairy calling, she found great fairy friends, too!

Right then, the kitchen door squeaked open and Garbanzo flew over to the center of the table. "Peaches said that Princess Itty wanted to see me," she said.

The Queen gave her daughter
a quick look. "Itty, you know not
to bother Garbanzo while she's
cooking—" her mom began.

"Oh, but this will be quick," Itty promised. She took out the present she'd hidden under her chair. "I made this for you!" Itty cried.

"Wow, a present? For me?" Garbanzo squeaked in surprise.

Itty nodded. Garbanzo excitedly tore off the kitty wrapping paper.

"What a beautiful spice rack!" Garbanzo exclaimed. "Thank you so much!"

"Why, you're *fairy* welcome," Itty replied. "Bree and I made it together. Thank you for always making the most delicious food."

"Oh, of course! It is my true fairy calling to cook for your family," Garbanzo replied. "And I'm glad Bree has found her calling." She wiped a few fairy tears.

"Itty, would you like to come into the kitchen and help us with dessert?" Garbanzo then asked.

"YES, PLEASE! With marshmallows on top!" Itty exclaimed with glee.

"Great, it's my special treat for tonight *only*," Garbanzo quickly added.

"Oh, Mom, Dad, can I please go with Garbanzo?" Itty purred.

The Queen nodded, but the King shook his head.

"I'm not sure," the King began in a serious voice.

"*What?*" Itty called out. Was her dad really going to say no?

"Let me finish, Itty," the King said, his eyes twinkling. "We should all help *together*!" he cried, waiting for Garbanzo to approve.

The head food fairy looked from Itty to the King and then let out a sigh.

"Oh, like father, like daughter," she mumbled. But Itty could see that Garbanzo was secretly smiling. And Itty smiled too. Her new friend, Bree, had found

her true fairy calling. Helping the food fairies make dessert was the sweetest way to end a perfect day!

Here's a sneak peek at Itty's next royal adventure!

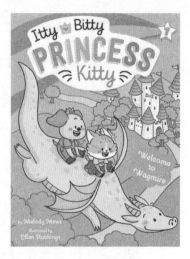

Princess Itty stood on the highest perch in the royal climbing room. The floor was a long way down! But Itty wasn't going to take one big jump. No, she was going to carefully plot a course and jump from one perch to another until she reached the ground. It was a new technique she had been practicing with her mom, the Queen of Lollyland.

While Itty's dad, the King, liked to take one big leap—and land with one big *thump!*—her mom preferred to work her way down by expertly jumping from one level to the next. It took a lot of skill, but it was the best and safest technique for a kitty with small paws like Itty.

A flash of movement outside caught Itty's attention. There was a dragon heading toward the palace! Actually, he was *rolling* toward the palace, because he was wearing roller skates.

A dragon on roller skates could only mean one thing!

Itty forgot all about being careful and leaped all the way down to the ground. She landed on the floor with a thump. She shook her paws and raced out of the climbing room.

"Mom! Dad! An announcement dragon from Wagmire is here!" Itty yelled as she raced through the grand hallway.

Her parents were already waiting at the palace doors.